EARTH KIDS

Written by ⭐ Jill Wheeler

Published by Abdo & Daughters, 4940 Viking Drive, Suite 622, Edina, Minnesota 55435.

Library bound edition distributed by Rockbottom Books, Pentagon Tower, P.O. Box 36036, Minneapolis, Minnesota 55435.

Edited by Julie Berg

LIBRARY OF CONGRESS CATALOGING-IN-PUBLICATION DATA

Wheeler, Jill C., 1964 -
    Earth kids / written by Jill Wheeler.
        p.   cm. -- (Target earth)
    Includes bibliographical references and index.
    Summary: Highlights the activities of several young environmentalists who are working to save our planet and suggests ways in which the reader can get involved.
    ISBN 1-56239-199-2
    1. Environmental protection -- Citizen participation -- Juvenile literature. 2. Environmentalists -- United States --Biogrpahy -- juvenile literature 3. Children -- United States -- Societies and clubs -- Juvenile literature. [1. Environmentalists. 2. Environmental protection. 3. Ecology.]   I. Title.   II. Series.
    TD171.7.W443   1993
    363.7'0525'092273--dc20
    [B]   93-15330
                                            CIP
                                          AC

Thanks To The Trees From Which This Recycled Paper Was First Made.

Table of Contents

Let's Begin Here.

In 1992, Church & Dwight Co., Inc., asked a group of fifth and sixth graders about the environment. The company asked the kids if they thought the world would be more polluted in the year 2000. Most kids said they thought it would be. The corporation also asked the kids if it frightened them to think about the Earth's future. More than half of the kids said it did.

It's not surprising kids worry about their future. The ozone layer is disappearing. Acid rain is killing lakes, streams and trees. People are running out of places to put the garbage they create. The Earth is losing many kinds of plants and animals, too. People can never replace these species.

Kids have a big reason to worry. They are the ones who will inherit the Earth. If the Earth is in bad shape, they will be in trouble, too. No wonder kids are some of the planet's best defenders.

All around the world, kids are making a difference. They are cutting waste in their schools. They are helping their families recycle. They are learning to be wise consumers. Kids have even formed their own environmental groups. These groups exchange ideas and information.

All of this activity is making the world a better place. And all of it is because of kids. In this book, we'll look at a few of these kids. We'll see what they did and why they did it. We'll also learn how everyone can become a defender of the planet.

Meet the Defenders

What have you done for the Earth lately? Here are the stories of some kids who can answer, "a lot!"

 **Melissa Poe**

Melissa Poe was nine years old when she watched a special episode of "Highway to Heaven" on television. The program showed how polluted the world could become. Melissa worried about what the pollution would do. She was afraid the pollution would hurt her. She was afraid it would harm her family, too. She wanted to stop pollution. So she wrote a letter to U.S. President George Bush. It read:

> Dear Mr. President,
>
> I want to keep on living till I am 100 years old.
> Right now I am 9 years old. My name is Melissa.
> You and other people, maybe you could put up
> signs saying: Stop Pollution, It's Killing the World.
> PLEASE help me stop pollution, Mr. President.
> Please, if you ignore this letter, soon we will die of
> pollution of the ozone layer.
> Please Help!
> Melissa Poe, Age 9
> Nashville, Tennessee

Melissa Poe

The president didn't write back. Melissa refused to give up. She had an idea.

She called an advertising company in her hometown of Nashville, Tennessee. She asked the company to put a copy of her letter on a billboard. The company helped put her letter on many billboards. People saw her letter and wrote to her.

Many children wrote to Melissa, too. She asked them to join her in working to stop pollution. She started a club called "Kids For A Clean Environment" (Kids FACE).

Kids FACE now has more than 30,000 members around the world. All of them are working to make a difference.

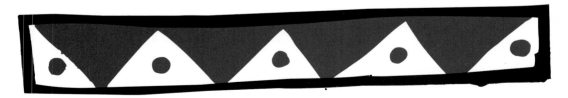

9

Christian Miller

Christian Miller was only seven years old when he found a dead sea turtle. The turtle was on the beach near his family's new home in Florida. Christian began finding dead turtles every week. He decided to do something to help.

Christian volunteered to help a local group clean beaches. He spent a year learning about sea turtles. At the end of the year, he received permission to rescue turtles.

Now, Christian often gets up early. He walks on the beach looking for turtle nests. He marks the nests where turtles lay their eggs so people don't step on them. Sometimes he finds baby turtles who need help getting to the sea.

He picks them up and puts them in the water. Sometimes he's too late and the turtles are dead.

On his computer, Christian keeps a record of what he does to help the turtles. The state of Florida uses the information to learn more about sea turtles.

Christian has saved more than 12,000 turtles over the past six years. His hometown of Palm Beach has honored him for his work. He also uses his work to write papers for school projects. That way, he can teach other kids about sea turtles and how people can help them.

Christian Miller

# Aruna Chandrasekhar

Aruna Chandrasekhar was in fourth grade when her teacher gave her class an assignment. The teacher asked everyone to write a book. The book was for a contest.

Aruna decided to write a book on the environment. She wanted to teach kids about the dangers of pollution. She decided to write about what oil spills do to harm animals. She had read a lot about the *Exxon Valdez* oil spill in Alaska. She knew how harmful pollution was to animals.

Aruna wrote about two sea otters trapped in an oil spill. In the book, people rescue the otters and clean them up. Readers learn all about what oil spills do to the Earth.

She called her book *Oliver and the Oil Spill*. It won first place in the contest. Thanks to Aruna, lots of children have learned about the dangers of oil spills.

Aruna Chandrusekhar

⭐ Courtney Collins ⭐

Fourteen-year-old Courtney Collins makes things happen. At the ripe age of ten, Courtney took it upon herself to do something about protecting the environment. She started by recruiting Children's Alliance for the Protection of the Environment (CAPE) founder Ingrid Kavanagh to speak to her elementary school classmates. The result: Courtney's school became the first CAPE school in Austin, Texas.

Since taking the first significant step three years ago, Courtney Collins, CAPE Ambassador, has traveled from the coasts of Oregon to the halls of government in Washington, D.C., to the home of the President of Mexico in Mexico City to carry her message: "We, the children, are going to grow up and live in this world. So we had better learn how to take care of it now."

May 1990 found Courtney at the podium in the General Assembly Hall of the United Nations. She shared the podium with several other CAPE Ambassadors, including the son of the President of Honduras. She related during her part of the address how the young Costa Rican CAPE members had captured her attention in Austin earlier that year.

On behalf of the worldwide members of the CAPE organization, Courtney accepted the United Nations Environment Programme's Global 500 Award in Mexico City. She was also selected in January 1992 to speak to the "CO_2 Challenge, Kids Coalition," chaired by Senators John Chaffee and Al Gore in Washington, D.C.

Courtney Collins

May 1992 found Courtney on the missionary trail again. She went to the 1992 United Nations Global Youth Forum in New York City. At this workshop she stressed the need for preserving the world's forests.

When she is not taking her message on the road, Courtney is working hard in her hometown of Austin. She helped organize a local lake cleanup. She worked with the U.S. Fish and Wildlife Service to establish the first Children's Forest within a sensitive area called Balcones Canyonlands National Wildlife Refuge. At the CAPE office Courtney answers letters from young environmentalists around the world who want to know what they can do to save their Earth now.

Kids Can Make A Difference.

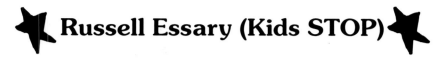

Russell Essary (Kids STOP)

Russell Essary remembers when he learned about the ozone layer. He was only five years old. It scared him to think the ozone layer would be gone someday. He decided to do something about it.

First, he wrote to environmental organizations. He asked for information on the ozone layer. The organizations sent him materials to read. He learned all about the ozone layer and why it was in danger.

Then Russell asked some friends at school to help him. They formed a group called "Kids Save the Ozone Project" (Kids STOP). There were 23 members.

A New York lawmaker heard about Kids STOP. He invited Russell and the other members to a meeting at city hall. At the meeting, the kids told everyone about the ozone problem. Newspapers and television stations wrote stories about what Russell and his group had done.

After the meeting, the lawmaker suggested a new law. The law would make people in New York recycle chlorofluorocarbons, or CFCs. CFCs are chemicals that eat away at the ozone.

Eventually, New York officials passed a law like Kids STOP wanted. Kids STOP then wrote letters asking other states and countries to ban CFCs, too. Many people listened. Russell even won an award from the president for his work.

Russell Essary

⭐ John Hegstrand ⭐

John Hegstrand began Sunny Hollow Elementary School in New Hope, Minnesota, as a new student in the sixth grade class. He made many new friends. But one friend he will never forget was Clinton Hill. Clinton cared about the Earth and wanted to make it new again. He founded Kids for Saving Earth (KSE) at Sunny Hollow shortly before his death at age 11 from cancer. In early 1990, John Hegstrand was chosen to represent KSE at the United Nation's youth forum in New York and presented a three-hundred-pound book with signatures of children from across the country.

John's next trip came in January of 1992. He was invited by the Children's Earth Fund to participate in a Senate hearing in Washington, D.C., with Senators John Chaffee and Al Gore. Twelve other kids from across the U.S. came together for the hearing.

The Senate hearing was centered around a project called the CO_2 Challenge. The project was set up to promote global awareness to prevent global warming. Thousands of kids from the U.S. signed a petition to reduce the amount of CO_2 they were using. They presented these signatures to the senators in hopes they would reach President Bush. Their goal was to convince the president to attend the Earth Summit in Rio de Janiero that coming June. The plan worked. John was excited to travel to Rio for the Earth Summit to represent children of the United States. There he voiced his concerns and feelings about our endangered planet with kids from other countries.

Important treaties were signed at the conference, paving the way for future treaties and a new awareness worldwide of the tasks ahead.

Currently John is working on a new project called "Plan-it for the Planet" as "senior advisor" to kids 12 years old and under at Nickelodeon Studios in Orlando, Florida.

John Hegstrand

Kids Against Pollution

The fifth grade class at Tenakill School in Closter, New Jersey, was studying the First Amendment. The First Amendment guarantees the right to free speech. Their teacher, Nick Byrne, assigned them to watch the news one weekend. He asked them to look for stories on important issues. On Monday, they were to discuss the issues they learned about.

When Monday came, many of the students talked about pollution. They had learned about pollution on New Jersey beaches, in landfills and in the air. The pollution made them angry. It also made them want to do something about it.

That morning they formed "Kids Against Pollution," or KAP. They also chose a motto. It was "Save The Earth, Not Just for Us, But for Future Generations."

KAP's first project involved air pollution. First, the students learned all they could about air pollution. They learned that CFCs are a big part of the air pollution problem. CFCs get in the atmosphere many ways. One way is when people make polystyrene, a kind of plastic foam.

Next, the students began writing letters. They sent letters to their local newspaper. The letters asked for a ban on polystyrene. The kids also wrote letters to other schools and asked the students to join KAP. They even wrote letters to the governors of New Jersey and New York.

People began to listen. The Tenakill school district banned polystyrene. Then, the town council of Closter banned polystyrene. Still, KAP knew there was more work to be done.

One of the biggest users of polystyrene was McDonald's Restaurants. McDonald's used hamburger boxes made with this material. KAP members decided to send a message to the company. They sent more than 3,000 letters to the company's headquarters. In the letters, they asked the company to stop using the boxes.

KAP members were not the only people pressuring McDonald's. Many other groups were asking the fast food chain to change, too. When everyone worked together, things began to happen.

In winter 1990, McDonald's officials announced they would help fight air pollution. By spring 1991, the company's 8,500 U.S. restaurants were using paper wrapping instead of foam boxes for hamburgers.

Today, there are more than 1,000 KAP chapters around the world. KAP members are also working with members of Congress. They are trying to pass an "environmental bill of rights" to further protect the environment.

⭐ Clinton Hill ⭐

Clinton Hill loved nature. He drew nature posters and wrote nature songs. He also worried about the future of the Earth. He was afraid many kinds of animals would be gone by the time he grew up.

Clinton decided that people were the solution to pollution. He also decided kids could show adults how to save the Earth. He started an informal club at his school. He called it "Kids for Saving Earth."

When Clinton was only 10 years old, he found out he was sick. He had a disease called cancer. Clinton began to wonder if he was sick because the Earth was getting sick, too. He wanted to work even harder to save the Earth. His parents promised to help him.

Clinton died when he was only 11 years old. His family remembered their promise to continue his mission. They started a formal chapter of Kids for Saving Earth (KSE) at Clinton's school. They made buttons and T-shirts from Clinton's drawings. They began a newsletter for club members. They even enlisted the help of Target Stores, a major corporation, to spread the word about KSE around the world.

"Give it a shot
when it's all you've got.
When everything seems
to be going bad:
just give it a shot
and you may start to get a lot.
Oh give it a shot
when it's all you've got."

Clinton Hill

Clinton Hill

25

KSE clubs quickly sprang up all over. Today, there are more than 565,000 KSE members around the world. All members take the KSE pledge when they join. The pledge is based on Clinton's ideas for saving the Earth. It goes like this:

The Earth's my home. I promise to keep it healthy and beautiful. I will love the land, the air, the water and all living creatures. I will be a defender of my planet. United with friends, I will save the Earth.

Get Into the Group

Kids can do a lot to help the environment. An easy way to make a difference is to be active in a group. You can start a group at your school or with your scout troop. Or there are many environmental groups for kids. Here's a list of some of them.

Children's Alliance for Protection of the Environment (CAPE) — CAPE has members around the world. The group publishes a newsletter to show kids how their lives affect the Earth. CAPE also gives ideas for activities kids can do. Write to them at P.O. Box 307, Austin, Texas 78767.

Children's Rainforest — The children in this group are working to protect a rainforest. The rainforests are in the country of Costa Rica in Central America. You can write to them at P.O. Box 936, Lewiston, Maine 04240.

Children for Old Growth — This is the group to be in if you love trees. Members work to save ancient forests. New members receive a forest poster and a newsletter. Their address is P.O. Box 1090, Redway, California 95560.

Friends of Wild Life (FOWL) — Learn how to start a wildlife club in your neighborhood. Write to FOWL at P.O. Box 477, Petaluma, California 94953.

Kids Against Pollution (KAP) — Learn how to stop pollution and get ideas from other members. Membership costs $15 a year. Write to KAP in care of Tenakill School, 275 High St., Closter, New Jersey 07642.

Kids For A Clean Environment (Kids FACE) — Join members around the world helping protect the Earth. Membership is free, and members get a newsletter. The address is P.O. Box 158254, Nashville, Tennessee 37215.

Kids For Saving Earth (KSE) — Keep Clinton Hill's dream alive by working to save the Earth. The KSE newsletter shares ideas from members around the world. Contact KSE at P.O. Box 47247, Plymouth, Minnesota 55447.

Kids in Nature's Defense (KIND) — KIND members work to slow global warming by saving energy. Start your own local group and receive the newsletter by writing to Patty Finch, 67 Salem Rd., East Haddam, Connecticut 06423.

Kids Save the Planet! (Kids STOP) — This group began to save the ozone. Learn how you can help with this and other issues. Send $2 in a self-addressed stamped envelope for project information. The address is P.O. Box 471, Forest Hills, New York 11375.

Target Earth —Target Earth is a study and reward program for schools sponsored by Target Stores. The program gives teachers lesson and activity ideas to help kids learn about the environment. Students get rewards when they complete the program. The Earthmobile is part of Target Earth. So is this book! To get involved, ask your teacher. Or write to us—the publisher of the Target Earth Earthmobile books! Abdo and Daughters Publishing, P.O. Box 36036, Minneapolis, Minnesota 55435.

Kids Can Make A Difference.

"Earth-Friendly" Magazines - Just For Kids

 P3: The Earth-Based Magazine for Kids — The P3 Foundation publishes this magazine. It costs $14 a year for 10 issues. You can subscribe by writing to them at P.O. Box 52, Montgomery, VT 05470.

 Ranger Rick — Ranger Rick costs $14 a year for 12 issues. The National Wildlife Federation publishes it. You can subscribe by writing to them at 1400 16th St. N.W., Washington, D.C. 20036-2266.

World — The National Geographic Society publishes a magazine especially for kids called *World*. It costs $12.95 a year and you'll receive 12 issues. The address is National Geographic Society, P.O. Box 2330, Washington, D.C. 20077-9955.

You can also learn more about the environment through a computer network. If you have a computer and a modem, ask a parent or teacher to help you. The National Geographic Society sponsors a computer network just for kids. For more information, write to the National Geographic Society, Educational Services, Department 1001, Washington, D.C. 20007.

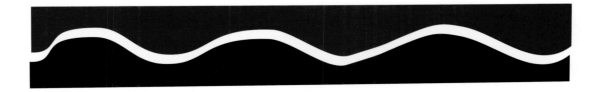

3 You Can Be a Defender, Too!

So you want to be a defender, too! There are many ways you can make a difference. Here are just some of the ways you can express your care for the Earth. You may even start your own environmental movement!

Make a bumper sticker that says "Save The Earth" or "Recycle." Use white adhesive-backed paper. Cut it into different shapes and decorate it. Make a sign and put it in your bedroom window where everyone can see it, too.

Does pollution make you angry? Do you wish people would stop cutting down the rainforests? Then do something about it. Write a letter to your elected officials. Tell them how you feel. Ask them to help save the Earth. If you need help finding out who to write to, ask a parent, adult friend or teacher.

Volunteer to write a paper in school about what kids can do to help save the Earth. Present your paper in class.

List all the items people can recycle. That can be everything from newspapers to clothes to toys. Make copies of your list on waste paper and pass them around to your friends. Encourage them to recycle as much as possible.

Get a group of your friends together to clean up a park or beach. Ask an adult friend, parent or teacher to work with you as an adviser. Have the adviser see if your group can plant some trees in your neighborhood.

Next time a friend invites you to a birthday party, give an eco-gift. Buy something reusable, like a book. Give something for the Earth, like a bird feeder. Wrap it in the comics section of an old newspaper. Ask your friend to recycle the newspaper. Or use leftover wrapping and bows from the holidays. (For more ideas, see the Target Earth Earthmobile book *Eco-Arts and Crafts*.)

Are you studying about the environment in school? If you're not, tell your teacher you want to. Write to your school, too. Tell the superintendent you think students should study the environment, too. And let them know about the Target Earth Earthmobile!

Bargain with your family. Say you'll unpack the groceries if they'll reuse the bags. Offer to organize boxes in the garage to collect items for recycling if they'll stop throwing recyclables in the trashcan.

Make a cassette or videotape. On it, tell how you feel about the environment. Tell what actions you'd like others to take to help. Send copies of your tape to your friends and to lawmakers.

Research environmental careers. You can be a defender of the planet when you're an adult, too. Start by reading the Target Earth Earthmobile book *Eco-Careers*.

Tell the world what you're doing. The organization "Renew America" wants to hear about what people are doing to save the Earth. Write to them about your community project. Their address is 1400 16th St. N.W., Suite 710, Washington, D.C. 20036.

Most of all, always act like an Earth Kid. People imitate what they see. If your friends see that you care about the Earth, they'll want to care, too. Read the next chapter to see if you're being a good example for others.

Are You
an Earth Kid?

It's important to talk about protecting the environment. It's even more important to do something about it. If you're doing something to save the Earth, you're an Earth Kid. Write to us and let us know (our mailing address is on page 29, under Target Earth). We may put your idea and your photo in a Target Earth Earthmobile book.

How much are you doing now? Take this quiz to find out. If you can answer yes to all questions, you're an Earth Kid. If you have some no's, see where you can improve.

Do You....

 Recycle at home?

 Recycle at school?

 Remind your parents to recycle?

 Look at packaging, then buy items with the least packaging?

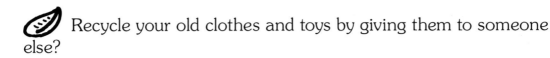 Recycle your old clothes and toys by giving them to someone else?

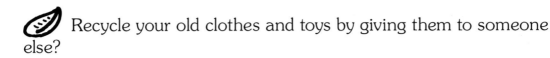 Ride your bike or walk whenever possible instead of asking for a ride?

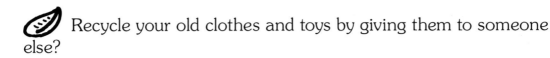 Turn off the lights when you leave a room?

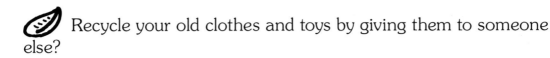 Wear a sweater instead of turning up the heat?

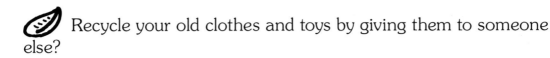 Re-use shopping bags?

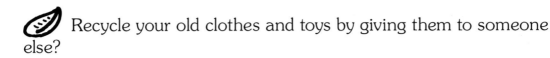 Buy only "dolphin-safe" tuna?

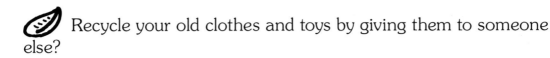 Use reusable containers instead of plastic wrap?

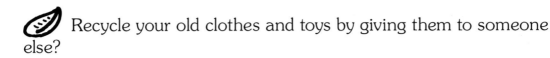 Turn off the water while brushing your teeth?

 Encourage all your friends to be an Earth Kid because...

Kids Can Make A Difference.

Glossary

Acid rain — pollution that mixes with clouds and falls back to the Earth in the form of rain.

Cancer — a harmful growth in the body. It can be caused by exposure to pollution.

Chlorofluorocarbons (CFCs) — a group of compounds that contain the elements carbon, chlorine, fluorine and sometimes hydrogen. They are used to make plastics and other solutions.

Exxon Valdez — an oil tanker that ran aground in Alaska.

Ozone layer — the upper layer of the Earth's atmosphere containing ozone gas that blocks out the sun's harmful ultraviolet rays.

Pollution — harming the environment by putting man-made wastes in the air, water and ground.

Polystyrene — a type of plastic made with CFCs. Foam hamburger boxes are made from this.

Rainforest — a woodland area that recieves 100 inches or more of rain a year.

Recycle — reusing materials instead of wasting them.

Sea turtle — a reptile that lives in the sea.

Species — a group of animals or plants that has certain characteristics in common.

Toxic — something poisonous.

Waste — worthless objects that are thrown away.

Connect With Books

Kid Heroes of the Environment by The Earth Works Group, edited by Catherine Dee, Earth Works Press.

50 Simple Things Kids Can Do To Save The Earth by the Earth Works Group, Andrews and McMeel.

Going Green: A Kid's Handbook to Saving the Planet, by John Elkington, Julia Hailes, Douglas Hill and Joel Makower, Puffin Books.

A Kid's Guide to How to Save The Planet by Billy Goodman, Avon Books.

It's My Earth, Too by Kathleen Krull, Doubleday.

Earthwatch - Earthcycles and Ecosystems by Beth Saran, Ph.D., Addison-Wesley Publishing Company.

Good Planets Are Hard To Find by Roma Dehr and Ronald M. Bazar, Earth Beat Press.

Save The Earth by Betty Miles, Alfred A. Knopf.

Index

TARGET EARTH™ COMMITMENT

At Target, we're committed to the environment. We show this commitment not only through our own internal efforts but also through the programs we sponsor in the communities where we do business.

Our commitment to children and the environment began when we became the Founding International Sponsor for Kids for Saving Earth, a non-profit environmental organization for kids. We helped launch the program in 1989 and supported its growth to three-quarters of a million club members in just three years.

Our commitment to children's environmental education led to the development of an environmental curriculum called Target Earth™, aimed at getting kids involved in their education and in their world.

In addition, we worked with Abdo & Daughters Publishing to develop the Target Earth™ Earthmobile, an environmental science library on wheels that can be used in libraries, or rolled from classroom to classroom.

Target believes that the children are our future and the future of our planet. Through education, they will save the world!

Minneapolis-based Target Stores is an upscale discount department store chain of 517 stores in 33 states coast-to-coast, and is the largest division of Dayton Hudson Corporation, one of the nation's leading retailers.